THE
Little Fellow

THE
Little Fellow

DRAWINGS BY *Diana Thorne*
STORY BY *Marguerite Henry*

HOLT, RINEHART AND WINSTON

NEW YORK · CHICAGO · SAN FRANCISCO

93579-0212

Printed in the United States of America

To
Marguerite Jupp,
who first introduced me to
The Little Fellow
at Joy Farm

Every morning the same thing happened to Chip. He opened his
eyes to find himself curled up on a bed of straw.

The straw was warm. In fact, it was so warm that Chip played
make-believe.

He closed his eyes and made believe he was still asleep.

Chocolate, his mother, knew he was only playing.

She rubbed her nose against Chip's. Then she began to lick him all over. That was a big job. It took her a long time.

First, she washed his face with her tongue. Then she washed his fuzzy coat. The more she licked, the fuzzier Chip's coat looked.

She even polished his tiny white hoofs with her tongue. It seemed as if she couldn't stop licking him.

But Chip did not mind. He could have stayed there forever, enjoying her warm washcloth of a tongue.

Once in a while Chip would nibble along his mother's silky neck.

Chocolate often nipped him too. Her teeth were e-nor-mous, but she was very gentle.

Chip's bath always made him feel frisky—AND hungry.

Because he was so hungry, he drank his mother's milk until his sides were as round as a barrel.

By this time in the morning Whitey could be heard, whistling softly as he went about his work.

Whitey filled the feed boxes and opened and closed the stalls.

He was exactly the same color as Chocolate, but still everyone called him Whitey.

Soon Whitey's shiny face appeared over the top of the stall.

"Mawnin', Miz Choclit," he grinned. "Lan' sakes! Dat foal ob yo's is growin' jes' lak a weed. Fack is, he's mos' nigh growed up. An' a thororbred ef I evah seed one! De white folks gwine be mighty proud o' yo' baby."

He stroked Chip's nose, then his neck, then his flanks. Chip loved to be petted by Whitey, although his hands were rough and horny.

Whitey poured some crushed oats into Chocolate's feed box.

"Yo-all turn yo' face away, Choclit," he said. "Dis li'l dab am for Chip."

Chip tasted the oats.

They were very dry. He decided he liked warm milk better.

"Now, den, Miz Choclit, *you* show de lil' fellah how to eat."

Chocolate did that very thing. With a noisy crunching, she cleaned up all the oats that Chip had left. She begged Whitey for more.

"Yas, sah!" chuckled Whitey. "Dat's de way to eat!"

Then he led Chocolate out into the warm sunshine.

Chip trotted by his mother's side, like a wobbly shadow.

There were five or six other horses in the pasture, but Chip was the only baby.

This was Chip's first spring. Never before had he heard birds sing. Never before had he seen pink clover.

He dipped his nose into a patch of the clover. He munched one or two of the bigger flowers.

"That's good!" he thought, as he chewed, "but I like milk better."

He sniffed the crab-apple blossoms in the distance. He ran. He jumped. He squealed. He bucked at nothing at all.

He was so happy that he rolled over on his back and kicked his legs wildly in the air.

How good it felt to get the very center of his back scratched!

In the midst of his rolling, he suddenly stopped and rested, his feet pawing the sky.

He could hear new, strange sounds now . . . the glug-glug of a bullfrog, the mewing of a catbird, the humming of a bee. Some day, when he had more time, he would find out where those noises came from.

A cottontail rabbit whiffed by, close to his whiskers. Chip was having too much fun, lying there in the sun, to chase him.

Instead he just snapped at him with his baby teeth. Then he snorted and whinnied fiercely.

This was LIFE.

Chip was making so much noise himself that he did not hear Chocolate calling him. She actually had to push him up with her nose to make him pay attention.

Chocolate and all the other horses began to gallop toward the fence.

"Cloppety! Cloppety!" went their big hoofs.

Chip hurried to catch up with them.

"Clippety! Clippety!" went his tiny hoofs.

There at the fence stood The Family.

This was the nicest time of day for Chocolate and Chip and all the other horses.

The Family always brought little treats with them.   There were carrots or red apples for the grown-up horses.

For Chip there was a lump of delicious sugar.

Chip did not know which he liked better—the sugar or the salty taste of The Man's hand.

First, he curled his lips around the sugar and ate that. Then he licked The Man's hand. He always nodded his head at the salty taste of it. And The Man always turned to The Ladies and said:

"See that? The Little Fellow wants more!"

Then everyone in The Family began to praise Chip.

"What bright eyes he has! And what lively ears!" exclaimed The Ladies.

"He will fly like the West Wind," said The Man. "He will bring honor to Bluebell Farm."

"I love the white star on his face and his neat white stockings," said one of The Ladies.

"Oh, feel his funny little whiskers and his fuzzy coat!" cried the other Lady.

"He will be strong. He will be swift," said The Man, with a far-away look in his eye.

The Family petted Chip. They stroked the white star on his nose. Their voices were soft and low, so Chip stood very still.

"Isn't he gentle?" asked The Ladies.

"He has fire and spirit," said The Man.

"He's a little beauty!" they all agreed.

Chip had no idea what they were saying. All he knew was that whatever they were talking about pleased him very much.

Often The Man sang as he and The Ladies walked back to the big house on the hill.

Chip pricked up his ears until they looked like tiny trumpets. He wanted to catch every bit of the nice sound the people made.

Even with all the attention he was getting, Chip was anxious to grow up.

He wanted to be as big as Chocolate and the other horses. He wanted to do what they did.

He wanted to bugle through his nose.

He wanted to sleep standing up.

He wanted to be able to enjoy cropping grass the way they did.

More than any of these grown-up manners, in fact, more than all of them put together, Chip wanted to brush flies with his tail. He did not want to do it the way a colt flaps his tail. He wanted to do it the grand, swishy way the grown-ups did.

The grown-ups made a regular ceremony of it!

Every noon when the sun was high in the sky, the big horses gathered in the shade of a honey locust tree. Then they chose partners and stood side by side.

What interested Chip was the way they stood. One partner always faced one way; the other faced the opposite way.

When the flies began to buzz, the horses' tails went SWISH! SWISH!

In that way each horse flicked the flies from his partner's face.

To Chip, this seemed wonderful.

He wanted to have a partner and to go SWISH! SWISH! with his tail.

Of course Chocolate let him stand close to her side, but she did all the swishing herself.

The minute Chip began to flap his tail, Chocolate walked away from him.

Chip wondered why she did this.

One day all the horses were napping in the shade of the honey
locust tree. Chip noticed one horse standing all by herself.

It was big Fanny Jenks.

She had no one at all to brush flies for her.

Chip watched her for some time. He saw a large horsefly crawl down her nose. Even when her head nodded as she dozed, the fly stuck on her nose.

Chip suddenly had an idea.

Little by little, he made his way over to Fanny Jenks. He was very quiet about it.

"This is going to be fun!" he thought. "Now *I* can be part of a team."

Softly, he put his front feet alongside Fanny's back feet. He stood side by side with big Fanny Jenks. Now he could chase flies for Fanny, and Fanny could chase flies for him.

"At last I can be grown-up!" he figured.

Chip forgot that he was just a little fellow.

He forgot that he was only half as tall as Fanny Jenks and only half as long as Fanny Jenks.

He didn't know that his tail was short and frizzly—AND THAT IT TICKLED!

For a minute or two there were no bug noises. Fanny Jenks kept right on snoozing.

Chip was beginning to think the whole idea rather tiresome.

Suddenly a fly zoomed down. This time it lighted right on Fanny's back.

SWISH! SWISH! went Fanny Jenks' tail. It felt silky as it brushed Chip's face.

FLAPPETY! FLAPPETY! went Chip's little brush of a tail. It didn't begin to reach Fanny Jenks' face. It just reached her forelegs. It tickled Fanny Jenks' legs.

With a wild snort, Fanny Jenks woke up. Chip could see the whites of her eyes and her ears laid back flat. He watched her wrinkle up her muzzle and show her big, yellow teeth.

For some reason Chip could not move. It was almost as if his hoofs were frozen to the earth.

But Fanny's were not. She wheeled round and kicked up her heels. Pieces of turf flew in Chip's face. He coughed and sneezed.

"Oh, OH!" he thought, "I'm going away from here." His legs began to move. He backed away as fast as he could and scampered over to his mother's side.

For the rest of the afternoon he stayed very close to Chocolate. He'd just let those flies bite Fanny Jenks all they wanted to. See if he cared!

About a week later Fanny Jenks had a surprise for the other horses.

When Whitey led her out to pasture, a brand-new baby foal trotted by her side.

Fanny neighed a cheery good morning to everyone. Then she pranced round the pasture as if she and her colt were on parade.

It was Chip's turn to snort now.

"Humph," he squeaked. "What a little thing! Why, he's so tiny he looks like a filly instead of a man-horse like me. He can't even keep his balance! His legs go scooting every which way."

Chip turned away with a tiny sneeze.

Just then Chip caught the sound of soft voices. His ears quivered. His heart began to beat faster.

Yes! Yes! It was The Family. Chocolate did not have to call Chip this time. Chip knew those voices well.

Oh, this was the best part of the day!

Chip could almost taste the sugar melting on his tongue.

He could almost feel the soft hands stroking his nose.

He could almost hear The Family say, "What a little beauty he is!"

The sound of those friendly voices was like the ringing of a dinner bell. The horses came galloping from all over the pasture.

"Cloppety! Cloppety!" went their big hoofs.

"Clippety! Clippety!" went Chip's tiny hoofs.

But Fanny Jenks' colt made scarcely any noise at all.

Chip crowded rudely up in front of the other horses. He nuzzled for the little morsel of sugar.

The Family was actually walking away from him. What had happened? They were moving toward Fanny Jenks' baby.

"No two ways about it," said The Man. "Here's a real colt!"

"His coat is red-gold," said one of The Ladies.

"We'll call him Strawberry Jenks," said The Man.

"What bright eyes he has! And what lively ears!" said The Ladies.

"He's a little beauty," they all agreed.

And the delicious sugar went to the *new* colt.

Poor Chip! All he got was a tiny piece of apple. It tasted sour.

He was so angry that he trembled.

"I will make The Family look at *me*," he decided. He stamped and pawed the earth. He raised his head and neighed sharply. To his complete surprise, he almost bugled through his nose.

But The Family just laughed and said, "Why I do believe The Little Fellow is jealous!"

Even the horses laughed.

This was too much.

Chip was so jealous that he hardly knew what he was doing. He sidled over to Strawberry Jenks. He nosed his way in between Fanny and Strawberry. Fanny was getting her share of the food, so she paid no attention to Chip.

Slyly, Chip nipped the baby colt with his teeth. It was just a little nip.

Then he completely forgot himself and took a big bite.

He hadn't meant to bite so hard. Or had he?

With a whinny of terror, Strawberry whirled round Chip and started for his mother.

"The big baby!" thought Chip. "For less than a turnip I'd chase him out of the pasture."

Quickly he blocked Strawberry's path and showed his sharp baby teeth.

Strawberry jumped like a cat out of a bag. Chip was after him in a flash. Behind him he could hear the sharp beat of hoofs—Fanny's, no doubt. She would be on him in a minute.

Strawberry was fleeing toward the fence.

On the other side of the fence The Family was running toward him.

All at once Strawberry stumbled and somersaulted into the air. He landed upside down between the planks of the fence.

Chip had to dig his hoofs into the turf to keep from piling on top of him.

Poor Strawberry was caught fast! He looked so funny there, squirming and pawing the air, that Chip laughed a little high horse-laugh.

It wasn't funny to Strawberry though. He squealed loudly for his mother.

Fanny Jenks ran to his side, nuzzling him and trying to push him up with her nose. The Family tried to help too.

The other horses came at a gallop from all over the pasture. The noise grew louder and louder. There were snortings, shrill cries, and baby whinnies. There were thump-thumpings of many hoofs. There were the worried voices of The Family. All these noises seemed mixed up together into one great noise.

Chip was amazed at all the trouble one little bite had caused.

At last Whitey came running. He spoke softly, soothingly, to Strawberry, and soon had him up on his long, wobbly legs.

Fanny was quieting him with her tongue and nickering to him. Then she nursed him.

He really wasn't hurt much. He was just frightened.

The minute Chocolate saw that Strawberry was all right, she began to push Chip with her nose. She pushed him hard. Chip could tell that she was angry. She was pushing him to the far end of the pasture.

When she had him alone, she started talking to him in little whinnies. Yet even while she scolded, she rubbed noses with him.

"Chip, my son," she nickered, "you must not be selfish. Where is your horse sense? Strawberry Jenks is just a baby. You're practically grown-up. This is a wide pasture, Chip. There is room for all."

Chip was thoroughly ashamed of himself now. He agreed with everything Chocolate said about him.

Yes, he knew he might have hurt Strawberry.

Yes, he knew Strawberry was only a baby.

Yes, he supposed The Family could like two colts equally well, as soon as the newness wore off Strawberry.

Chocolate had never scolded Chip before. He was feeling more ashamed of himself by the minute. If only he did not have to face the other horses!

With his head low and his tail tucked in, he walked away very slowly.

He wished that it was night and that he could hide in the darkness of his stall. He cried little colt cries. Then he snuffled. No one seemed to care for him any more. He felt very much alone.

Chip was miserable for days. Sometimes even his mother seemed to be more interested in Strawberry Jenks than she was in him.

Often he would notice her ears moving back and forth to catch everything The Family said about him.

At night, Chip began to roll about in his stall.

"Laws a'massy!" said Whitey. "Is he gwine be a tumblebug all his life?"

Horses that roll in their stalls are called tumblebugs. No horse likes to be called a tumblebug.

"Tumblebug, my eye!" thought Chip.

The days were growing much warmer now, and the pasture was a dark green carpet.

Young Strawberry Jenks sometimes left his mother's side and went off on little exploring trips. He even tried to be friends with Chip.

Try as Chip would, he could not be friendly with Strawberry. Instead, he would kick up his heels and run away. Then he would snort at Strawberry.

One hot July morning when the flies began to buzz and bite earlier
than usual, the horses stopped grazing in the sun.

Lazily they walked over to the shade of the honey locust tree.

"Clop! Clop!" went their big hoofs.

"Clip! Clip!" went Chip's little hoofs.

Strawberry Jenks made scarcely any noise at all.

It was cool and restful in the shade. The grown-up horses were standing in twos. Some drowsed. Some just looked off into the distance and sniffed.

Chip noticed that his mother had chosen Fanny Jenks as a partner.

Fanny was brushing flies for Chocolate, and Chocolate was brushing flies for Fanny.

SWISH! SWISH! went their tails.

Chip was left all by himself.

Suddenly a warm body rubbed against his own. How nice and fuzzy it felt!

Without looking round, he knew it was Strawberry Jenks.

"Why, my stars!" thought Chip, "Strawberry is almost as tall as I am. He is almost as long as I am. He is *practically* the right size."

Just then a couple of big horseflies came buzzing along.

FLAPPETY! FLAPPETY! went Chip's short curly tail.

And FLAPPETY! FLAPPETY! went Strawberry's short, frizzly tail.

Chip nickered softly.

"Why, Strawberry Jenks is all right! He's all right!"

Back and forth flapped Chip's tail.

Back and forth flapped Strawberry's tail.

Away flew the pesky flies.

Chip was mighty proud of himself. He was taking care of Fanny Jenks' baby. He had actually taught Strawberry how to brush flies!

At last he was happy. At last he could brush flies like the grown-up horses! At last he was a partner!

Chip quivered with delight. He licked Strawberry's leg, and this time he took just a friendly little nip for the fun of it.

"Chocolate was right," thought Chip. "There *is* room for all." And he let out a small whinny of happiness into the drowsy summer noon.